You know how to love

Words by RACHEL TAWIL KENYON
Pictures by MARY LUNDQUIST

PHILOMEL

PHILOMEL BOOKS

An imprint of Penguin Random House LLC, New York

First published in the United States of America by Philomel Books,
an imprint of Penguin Random House LLC, 2020.

Text copyright © 2020 by Rachel Tawil Kenyon. Illustrations copyright © 2020 by Mary Lundquist.

Penguin supports copyright. Copyright fuels creativity, encourages diverse voices, promotes free speech, and
creates a vibrant culture. Thank you for buying an authorized edition of this book and for complying with
copyright laws by not reproducing, scanning, or distributing any part of it in any form without permission. You
are supporting writers and allowing Penguin to continue to publish books for every reader.

Philomel Books is a registered trademark of Penguin Random House LLC.

Visit us online at penguinrandomhouse.com

Library of Congress Cataloging-in-Publication Data is available.

Manufactured in China.

ISBN 9780593114575

1 3 5 7 9 10 8 6 4 2

Edited by Talia Benamy.
Design by Ellice M. Lee.
Text set in Adobe Jenson Pro.

The artwork for this book was made with pencil, watercolor, and gouache on watercolor paper.

For Dani and Zach, you are my best things.
For David, you are my us.
—RTK

To Courtney and Adam, two people who definitely know
how to love. Thank you for all the love and support.
—ML

It starts at the start
when you can't even talk.
Before you stand up
and learn how to walk.

Deep in your heart,
the knowing is there.
You know how to love
and you know how to care.

Then as you get bigger
and start to explore,
without even trying
you learn to do more.

You learn how to listen
and hug and be kind.
And help someone out
when they're falling behind.

You go on adventures
and learn how to share.
And when you play games,
you always play fair.

And just as you grow,
the knowing grows too.
You'll see someone hurting
and know what to do.

You'll offer your smile
and share your space.
You'll make someone's world
a safe, peaceful place.

When someone's excluded,
left out in the cold,
you'll reach out and offer
your strong hand to hold.

During your journey
some days will seem tough.
You'll wonder if all that
you know is enough.

You may not be sure
each minute, each day,
of just what to do
or just what to say.

So take a deep breath
and look to your heart.
Remember the things
you knew at the start.

There are all sorts of people,
as many as stars.

Just give them a chance,
and learn who they are.

You'll find some are funny,
some quiet, some tall.
Some look like you,
and some not at all.

Some like to color
and some like to dance.
They may teach you how
if you give them a chance.

If they don't feel like sharing,
that's also okay.
Not everyone feels like it
every day.

But if you take care
to be thoughtful and strong,
you'll find that you too
have a place you belong.

What once was so small,
deep in your heart,
has been growing in there,
right from the start.

You have the power
like waves in the ocean.
Use what you know
to put love in motion.

Wherever life takes you,
wherever you go,
trust what's inside you
and let kindness flow.

DEC U 7 2020

Dauphin County Library System
Harrisburg, Pennsylvania